First Little Readers™

E

Little Red Hen Makes a Pizza

by Liza Charlesworth

ISBN: 978-1-338-29788-1

Illustrated by Tammie Lyon

First printing, June 2018.

 Published by Scholastic Inc. Printed in Jiaxing, China.

Here is Little Red Hen.
"I will make a pizza," she said.
"Cluck, cluck, cluck!"

Here are her friends,
Pig and Cow and Horse.
Will they help?

"Pig, will you help me
put on the sauce?" she asked.
"No, I am too busy," said Pig.
"Oink, oink, oink!"

So Little Red Hen said,
"I will do it all by myself.
Cluck, cluck, cluck!"

"Cow, will you help me
put on the cheese?" she asked.
"No, I am too busy," said Cow.
"Moo, moo, moo!"

So Little Red Hen said,
"I will do it all by myself.
Cluck, cluck, cluck!"

"Horse, will you help me
put on the mushrooms?" she asked.
"No, I am too busy," said Horse.
"Neigh, neigh, neigh!"

So Little Red Hen said,
"I will do it all by myself.
Cluck, cluck, cluck!"

Little Red Hen put the pizza
in the oven.
Bake, bake, bake!

Little Red Hen took the pizza
out of the oven.
The kitchen was messy,
but the pizza smelled yummy!

Pig and Cow and Horse
came running.
"Oink! Moo! Neigh!" they said.
"Can we help you
eat the pizza?"

Little Red Hen said,
"I should say NO
because you did not help.
But I will say YES
because I like to share."

So Pig and Cow and Horse
helped eat the pizza.

Yummy, yummy!
Yummy, yummy!

Then Pig and Cow and Horse
cleaned up the mess.
Why?
Because Little Red Hen
was too busy!